WILLIAM TELFORD

ALFREDO & ME

STOAT BOOKS

ALFREDO & ME

ISBN: **978-1-918724-02-8**

POCKET SERIES

02

First published 2026

Edited by Leona Franke

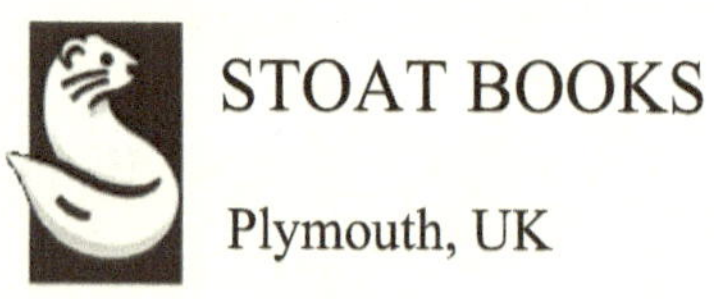

WILLIAM TELFORD

Alfredo & Me is a tragicomedy of football, fame, and fragile identity, told through the eyes of a Hungarian striker lost in the shadow of Alfredo Di Stéfano at Real Madrid. William Telford writes with wit, bite, and affection, capturing the absurd collisions of ego and admiration, cultural displacement and the need to matter.

This is a story shaped by comic excess, bittersweet rivalries, and the quiet despair of always being second best. Through diary entries rich with satire and pathos, *Alfredo & Me* unpicks what it means to worship and resent in the same breath. There are no fairytale victories here — only bruising laughter, small betrayals, and flashes of tenderness in the glow of borrowed greatness.

OTHER BOOKS:

How Love Works, 2020

ALFREDO
& ME

SEPTEMBER 1, 1958 - A day I shall not forget. The first at my new job, and I feel I have arrived at last. Here I am, finally, at the summit of my profession; the pinnacle, the penthouse suite, the vertiginous peak. For me, no more wasting precious time in Budapest or Bologna, I have arrived - at Real Madrid.

And what a welcome. The boss was there himself to greet me. Not the Generalissimo, of course, I mean the great Señor Santiago Bernabéu. A snow-topped mountain of a man, so imperious, he shook my hand with all the warmth of the Castilian sun.

'Señor,' he said. 'You are the most welcome guest of this great family of Real Madrid Club de Fútbol. Tequila? Or vino? How about some Sangria?'

'*Non gracias*,' I replied. 'I must watch my waistline.'

We both laughed.

'Tomorrow,' he said. 'You shall meet your team-mates.'

'*Manana*,' I answered.

SEPTEMBER 2 - I have ascended to heaven. By that I mean the architectural splendour and beauty of the capital and, undoubtedly, its greatest edifice: the Bernabéu Stadium itself. Like its founder, it is imposing, towering over me, the pristine angles and curves of its construction glinting in the Iberian daylight. And as if to confirm my elevation to divinity, I was soon surrounded by a flock of angels, my new comrades, all in pure white, a celestial choir, with football boots instead of wings.

There was the goalkeeper Rogelio Domínguez, as handsome as Gregory Peck, the centre-half, José Santamaría, powerful like a Pamplona bull; Paco Gento, who can talk as fast as he can run, and the elegant Raymond Kopa, who kissed me on both cheeks and whispered, '*Bonjour*'.

Then the gleaming mass parted to afford my first glimpse of the archangel himself: Alfredo di Stéfano, who strode towards me silently, his feet making no sound on the baked turf. Was that the sun reflecting off his denuded crown, or a halo?

The great man took my hand, shook it manfully, and kissed it delicately, may I say even femininely.

'I am honoured to meet you, Señor di Stéfano,' I said.

'Nonsense,' he asserted. 'It is I who am honoured. Be my guest tomorrow for dinner, Frankie. Paella? Or pasta? How about lasagna?'

'*Gracias*,' I said. 'But I have to keep an eye on my waistline. And it's Ferenc, not Frankie.'

We both laughed.

'Tomorrow,' he said. 'I shall show you the treasures of Madrid.'

'*Hasta manana,*' I answered.

What a lovely man.

SEPTEMBER 3 - How far I have come from the muddy fields of Kispest. Madrid is even more marvelous than I imagined. And what a host Alfredo is. The Royal Palace, the Teatro Real with its 100-year-old opera house, and the national library, we explored them all in just one morning.

And everywhere we went people rushed up to him to shake his hand, kiss his cheeks, pat his back, grovel at his feet, laugh and cry in equal measure. I could not be in more exalted company if I was being escorted by the Generalissimo and young Juan Carlos. Alfredo has time for everyone, a true hero and man of the people. And so generous, with his money and his mind. After a huge lunch of steak followed by ice cream, which he insisted on paying for, but ate very little of himself, I noticed, he took me to the Prado where he personally explained the history of the building and the works within. Alfredo seems to be an expert in Velázquez and Goya and can expound for hours on their lives and works.

'You have nothing like this in Budapest,' he said proudly.

'We have many fine galleries,' I answered.

'Yes, but nothing like this,' he said again.

And he's right, we have nothing like this, and we have no one like Alfredo either, even if he does still insist on calling me Frankie.

SEPTEMBER 5 - A fabulous training session. I thought the Hungarian side of 1952 to 1954 was good, but, with respect to my countrymen, they are nothing compared to my current companions. And first amongst them is Alfredo. What a wizard. He moves like a snake, and stings like a hornet. Not for nothing do they call him the greatest footballer in the world. And perhaps he is also the greatest man in the world.

After training, he took me to a restaurant near the Chamartín training ground and bought me a huge meal of pork and potatoes, with trifle to follow. During my feast, of which he again partook very little, Alfredo gave me a potted history of his home city, Buenos Aires, and a less than potted recount of the political upheavals of South America since 1700, with particular attention to his homeland's struggle for independence from his current country of residence.

'A far more red-blooded story than that of Hungary's,' he insisted, to which I reminded him of the 1848 resistance to Habsburg rule.

‘A minor disturbance,’ he intoned. ‘Did the Danube run red with the blood of martyrs, like the Río de la Plata during the naval war off Montevideo?’

I told him I didn’t know, but was fairly sure that some people got hurt, as I reached for another bowl of trifle. Alfredo is so well informed, so educated. I am in awe.

SEPTEMBER 14 - At last, into action. Real trounced Athletic Bilbao, and Alfredo was magnificent. He travels like the wind through a pine forest, weaving and never slowing. Every touch of the ball is executed with the deftness of a surgeon or, dare I say it, Picasso with his brush. Alfredo is like a vision, a Manchego-white ghost, and after he scored, I congratulated him and said, '*Señor*, you are truly our king, lynchpin and trump card.'

'Nonsense,' he retorted. 'We are a team, albeit one with a great player. But a team no less, Frankie.'

How true. But I wish he wouldn't call me Frankie.

SEPTEMBER 21 - I have scored at last, and then some - a hat trick. Against poor, unfortunate Sporting de Gijón, I was lucky enough to be in the right place at the right time to punish three lapses of concentration. I have always been a goal-scorer and do not intend to let my average slip. My teammates celebrated my fortune, and I was carried off the pitch on the mighty shoulders of Mateos and Santamaría.

Alfredo, whose willowy form seemed unfazed by the rigours of the game, gave me his personal seal in the changing room.

'Congratulations,' he said. 'I knew you would score eventually.'

'It's my second game,' I said, somewhat puzzled.

'Exactly,' he answered.

'Alfredo,' I quickly rebounded, 'I will dedicate my hat-trick to you. We are so alike. Both 32 years of age, both exiles and both great goal-scorers.'

'A slight correction,' he butted in. 'You are a great goal-scorer, whereas I am merely a great player.'

And then he offered to buy me supper.

JANUARY 1, 1959 - A new year already. Time has flown on swift wings. My four months in Madrid have been a blur of rampant victories and cultural delights. Thanks to Alfredo, we are leading the league and progressing in the European Cup. He is playing better than I could dream, and I am scoring regularly. The strange thing is my goals never seem to come from his passes. In fact, he rarely gives me the ball.

‘We play in different spheres,’ is how he put it. ‘I pull the strings, others dance. And you, Frankie, you tidy things up.’

Still, he has been most generous to me. Last week he showed me the Royal Palace, never letting me forget that Latin architecture is the finest on the planet. I pointed out to him that Budapest has some notable buildings, not least the third largest church in Hungary.

‘Size isn’t everything,’ he sniffed, and handed me an enormous bar of chocolate.

JANUARY 4 - God has been bountiful. Today we beat Las Palmas by 10 goals to one. Alfredo scored three, as did I. A telegram arrived, after the game, from the Generalissimo. It mentioned Alfredo but not me.

'Frankie sounds too much like Franco, he probably didn't want to confuse anyone,' explained Alfredo.

'It's Ferenc,' I asserted. 'You're still calling me Frankie.'

'I do apologise,' Alfredo said, giving a small bow. 'Would you like a piece of cheese? Adarga de Oro, a Spanish delicacy made with pasteurised cow's, goat's and sheep's milk. Hungary is not known for its cheese, is it?'

'Eh, no,' I replied. 'But the village of Kecskemét is vying to change that.'

'Stick to goulash,' he said, somewhat haughtily.

APRIL 5 - Alfredo has been behaving very strangely. At training he insists on taking all the free kicks, corners, and throw-ins. And he keeps informing us about how he won the Copa América with Argentina in 1947.

'Had it not been for the war in Europe, we'd have lifted the World Cup,' he said.

I reminded him that I won a gold medal with Hungary at the 1952 Helsinki Olympics.

'Ah, the Olympics,' he said. 'Isn't that for amateurs?'

I think I'm starting to go off Alfredo.

APRIL 7 - We have beaten our great rivals Atlético Madrid to progress to the European Cup final in Stuttgart. You'd think that would make everyone happy. Alas, this is not the case. Consecutive defeats have allowed our other great rivals, Barcelona, to overtake us in the league, and we are out of the Copa del Rey. The press are making an issue of my weight, saying I'm as slow as the Manzanares at its confluence with the Jarama. And Alfredo is not giving me the ball.

‘I play it to where you should be only to find out you are not there,’ he explained. ‘Perhaps you should eat less cheese and chocolate, and lay off the steaks.’

That made me so angry I almost dropped my rum baba.

MAY 7 - Disaster. I have strained a muscle and will miss the European Cup final. I was trying to retrieve a chocolate covered almond that Alfredo had given me during a break in training when I bent down all too suddenly and felt something snap around my midriff. The club doctor has recommended a month's rest. I am disconsolate.

Alfredo, on the other hand, is ecstatic.

'Never mind,' he said. 'When I score our winning goal, I will dedicate it to my great friend Frankie.'

'You're all heart,' I replied, almost choking on the almond.

MAY 11 - I am beginning to think that Alfredo is not my friend after all. He has taken to espousing the virtues of

Latin cinema now, and spent all of today telling me how ingenious Luis Buñuel is. He is also, it appears, a world authority on the French Nouvelle Vague.

'We have some fine young film makers in Budapest too,' I reminded him, though not being able to recall any of their names.

'Yes, but it is less a Nouvelle Vague and more something that is vaguely nouvelle,' he quipped.

Sometimes I want to pull out what's left of his golden hair.

JUNE 3 - My blackest day. Real Madrid have won their fourth consecutive European Cup. But without me. And, naturally, 47 minutes in, Alfredo scored our second goal.

The players were all over him, the press were all over him, even American film actress Gina Lollobrigida was all over him. No one can tell me what she was doing in our changing room, but she was there.

The Generalissimo sent Alfredo a bouquet and bottle of the finest

Champagne and Señor Bernabéu has given him exclusive use of his chalet in the mountains this summer.

All I got was a slice of Black Forest Gateau at the after-match banquet and even then, I had to sit at a table with our beaten rivals from Reims. I wouldn't have minded the break from Alfredo and his trumpeting, but the Frenchmen only wanted to talk about the damned Nouvelle Vague and ask me if there were any famous cheeses in Hungary.

Afterwards I decided to have it out with his holiness, 'Saint Alfredo', and so I apprehended him by the latrines.

'You never pass to me, and you have encouraged me to put on weight and get injured,' was the gist of my argument.

'I have done no such thing,' he countered. 'You see Frankie, you've only been at my club for one season, you've only been in my city for nine months, the cultural shock was always going to affect your performances. I'm sure you'll have better luck next year.'

'Cultural shock? Cultural shock? What on earth do you mean?' I spluttered.

'Frankie, dear boy, you are now in the land of Arriaga, of Pedrell, of Albéniz, not the backwater that produced Bartók and Liszt.'

'Budapest a backwater?' I coughed. 'And how dare you compare those three, er, er, dilettantes to the great Franz and Béla? You, you, baldy!'

'Me a baldy?' yelled Alfredo. 'That's fine coming from you, fatso!'

And with that, I drew on all my training as a major in the Hungarian Defence Force and launched a full-blooded assault on my bare-pated opponent. Unfortunately for me, I still had a rather large plate of rice pudding in my left hand, and, it turns out, Alfredo is a world class exponent of the martial art of Ju Jitsu and soon had me in a painful arm-lock with my face buried deep in the dessert.

'Submit, submit!' I yelled.

'I thought I was winning?' queried Alfredo.

'You are, I submit,' I screamed.

The club doctor says I shall have to have another four day's rest.

JUNE 10 - Last game of the season and I make a dramatic return to the team. My injuries, the ones inflicted both by the chocolate almond and by Alfredo, have healed and I joined my nemesis on the field against lowly Granada. For such a humble team, they put up a mighty fight and were holding us at one apiece with two minutes to go, when I changed the course of the game. Receiving the ball about 25 yards out I dribbled around two defenders and sidestepped the goalkeeper leaving the empty net at my mercy.

But then I saw Alfredo, standing on the edge of the six-yard box. I looked at him and his receding hair and his lined face and thought about the damage he had inflicted on me, physically and emotionally, and how he had insulted my city and country, its composers, architects, generals, filmmakers and cheese. And I looked at the empty goal, and remembered that I had 29 strikes this season, and so did he - and so I rolled the ball… straight to him.

Alfredo tapped it home and turned away to be enveloped in the grateful and loving arms of our teammates.

After the game Alfredo approached me in the changing room, took my hand, shook it manfully, and kissed it delicately, may I say even femininely, and said,

'Well played, Ferenc. You know, I'm looking forward to next season, I think you and I will forge a splendid partnership, inspire a great team, who knows, perhaps the greatest this sport has ever seen.'

And then he put his arm around my shoulder, gave a gentle squeeze, and, later, he smiled at me as we shared a large dish of chocolate mousse washed down, naturally, with a bottle of Secastilla, vintage 1949.

'Uh, uh,' he said, wagging his finger, as I went to refill my glass, and collect a second helping of pudding. 'You must watch your waistline.'

'Of course,' I said, putting down my plate. 'Whatever you say.' What a wonderful man Alfredo is.

www.ingramcontent.com/pod-product-compliance
Lightning Source LLC
LaVergne TN
LVHW051023080826
845145LV00009B/2772

* 9 7 8 1 9 1 8 7 2 4 0 2 8 *